HUSK

HUSK

A NOVELLA

RACHEL AUTUMN DEERING

TINY BEHEMOTH PRESS

Published by Tiny Behemoth Press

Columbus Ohio

TINY BEHEMOTH PRESS, MARCH 2016

All rights reserved. Published worldwide by Tiny Behemoth Press, Columbus Ohio.
Originally published by Thunderstorm Books.

ISBN-13: 978-0692661598
ISBN-10: 0-692-66159-X

www.rachelautumndeering.com

Cover painting by Tyler Jenkins
Cover design by Rachel Autumn Deering

To my dear friend, Kevin. Thank you for allowing me to tell your story.

And to my loving wife. Thank you for everything else.

"When common objects become charged with the suggestion of horror, they stimulate the imagination far more than things of unusual appearance."

—Algernon Blackwood, *The Willows*

"I want you to believe...to believe in things that you cannot."

—Bram Stoker, *Dracula*

HUSK

I

A MIGHTY ROAR

KEVIN BROOKS HAD TASTED BLOOD BEFORE, BUT NOT QUITE like this. He remembered the bitter, electric tang licked from a freshly picked scab when he was a kid, or the stinging flood that washed over his palate after he bit his cheek. This was different. This was something entirely new. He choked and gagged as the thick liquid hit the back of his tongue and slid down his throat. He tried to spit but his face was mostly covered with the stuff, so every time his tongue touched his lips, he drew more of it into his mouth. He swore he could taste the confusion, the anxiety, the shock, and the absolute terror. He wanted to vomit, but he found his stomach empty and his whole body racked with pain, lurching and jerking as he retched.

The high noon sun dominated the sky and baked the infertile earth in the remote southeastern Paktika province of Afghanistan. Troops running missions here grew used to the harsh conditions over time, but they never understood how so many people could call this place home. A line of heavily armored mine-detection vehicles driven by members of the 201st Engineer Battalion crept along the sandy desert road on a routine clearance mission, ensuring safe passage for a supply caravan coming into Forward Operating Base Kushamond. Bomb patrol didn't come with the most honor or recognition, but it kept the bank accounts growing back home.

The view along their route was unchanging and tedious, with miles of undulating dirt mounds far off in the distance to their left and spots of Kochi settlements—herds of goats and temporary shelters situated along the banks of dry river beds—on their right. The sameness of it all played tricks on their minds and hours seemed to stretch on into eternity. The previous day had seen a string of roadside explosive strikes which rendered two of their vehicles inoperable, an MRAP and a husky. Kevin was towing one of the battered beasts behind his wrecker and the other was loaded onto a camouflaged flatbed M-916 semi in front of him.

As the convoy snaked through the scorched landscape, Kevin's mind began to drift. It was Halloween, and all he wanted was to be back home, watching a marathon of The Munsters or handing out junk food and comics to the few neighborhood kids who still bothered to get dressed up and go door-to-door. He thought about the broke-dicks back at his home FOB, Orgun-E, and wondered what kind of goofy shit they were getting up to. As much as they pissed off the brass, he had warmed up to a couple of the goofier Joes. He couldn't help it, they were funny.

"Wake up, Wrench." A call came over the net. Kevin recognized the gravelly-voiced speaker as Platoon Sergeant Keene. A serious man, or at least that's the impression he intended to give.

"Sir," Kevin responded. He never knew why Sgt. Keene insisted on addressing him by his call sign. Route clearance wasn't exactly a secret squirrel mission.

"Got a husky stuck up here. Buried in the goddamn sand up to her tits. Drop your load and bring the wrecker down front to assist."

"Copy."

"Bravo 16, cover Wrench's nine and pull security."

"On the move."

The wrecker pulled out of its place in line and rolled toward the front of the convoy, followed closely by the Bravo 16 gun truck. Kevin squinted against the sun, watching the passing trucks on his right until he came to the mired semi. It was stuck all right, but that wasn't anything unusual for heavy equipment traveling the loose dirt roads in this region. He smiled and adjusted his microphone.

"I thought you had to have a license to drive one of those things."

"Eat shit, Brooksie. Just get us the fuck outta here, would ya?"

Kevin pulled his truck up past the M-916 and backed it into place. He nodded at the driver of the gun truck as it rolled to a stop beside him.

"Wrench and Bravo 16 in position."

"Copy that, Wrench. Dismount. Bravo 16 assistant gunner, get out there and help expedite the situation,"

Keene said. "I'd like to get moving again before supper time."

Assistant gunner Derrick Walton hummed a song to himself as he climbed down the ladder from the top of the gun truck. He was tall and skinny with red, sun-burned ears that stuck out from the sides of his head and freckles for days. He would be the first to admit he was probably not what most folks would call handsome, but he had enough charm and confidence to pull it off. The other kids on the track team had nicknamed him Opie because of his striking resemblance to the young Ron Howard character on The Andy Griffith Show. He liked to joke he was a solid five and a half. Most days.

"Howdy princess! You need a big, strong man to help you down out of that ol' truck?" Derrick asked. Kevin had always been the more athletic of the two, and outweighed Derrick by at least 40 pounds. All muscle.

"Macho man! Flex for me just a little bit."

"I ain't the type to show off, now. You know that. I'll flex my brains for you, make sure you don't do nothing stupid." Derrick opened one of the utility boxes mounted on the side of the wrecker and fished out a length of chain, hand over hand, letting it coil on the ground at his feet like a rusted serpent.

"Brains, he says! I swear, if brains was leather, you wouldn't have enough to saddle a junebug."

"Says the damn genius that talked me into coming over to this godawful place. If not for you, I'd be sitting at home right now with high speed internet and an endless supply of porn, jacking off into a clean sock. Heaven!"

Kevin grabbed the end of the chain from Derrick's hand and started walking toward the semi, dragging the metal links behind him.

"Yeah, well, cut me some slack, Tinkerbell. I thought maybe you would have grown a damn pair by now. God forbid you make something of yourself." Kevin turned on his heels to face Derrick and started walking backward, still dragging the chain. With his free hand, he pointed to a spot off to the side of the truck. "That's fine, you just stand over there and beat your bologna, and I'll get us back on the road."

"Hey, you know I'm just fooling with you about enlisting, right? I'm glad to be out here playing in this great big, hot-as-shit, why-does-this-fucking-place-even-exist sandbox with you."

The two had been best friends since elementary school, so Kevin was happy to have the company, even if Derrick was mostly useless when it came time to do any heavy lifting. The dynamic between them had always been the same, Kevin made sure the meatheads never gave Derrick too much shit and Derrick made sure Kevin didn't take life too seriously.

"I just bet you are." Kevin turned and started walking forward.

"Oh, hey! Happy Halloween, man." Derrick said, jogging to catch up.

"Thanks. It's fucked up I gotta spend my favorite day of the year in this shithole country with ungrateful peckerwoods like you."

"You going trick-or-treating later?"

"Why yeah. You think the brown shoes at Kushamond give out full size candy bars?"

"Doubtful. I'd settle for an MRE and a reach-around, though. Can't be picky." A big, fake smile stretched across Derrick's face and he jabbed Kevin in the ribs with his elbow.

Kevin kneeled in the sand near the M-916 and looped the heavy chain through the vehicle's front bumper. Derrick stood above him and scanned the horizon.

"Wanna hear a joke?" Kevin asked.

"I don't know. Do I?"

"It don't matter, you're fixing to hear one. Ready? These two old dried up fish meet on top of an Afghanistan mountain. One fish looks at the other one and says 'Hey, friend. Long time no sea.'"

"Well ain't that just the cutest thing I ever heard," Derrick said. "You get that one off an ice cream stick or a bubblegum wrapper?" Derrick waved his hand in front of his face, fanning the air around his nose as if he'd smelled something awful. "Your sense of humor is plumb rotten. I'll allow you an A for effort, though."

"I'll allow you an A for asshole. Let's hear you do one better."

"Well, a whopper like that won't be easy to follow, but I'll give 'er a shot. Knock, knock."

"You serious right now? You're gonna outdo me with a damn knock, knock joke?"

"C'mon, man. Just humor me. Knock, knock."

"All right, who's there?"

All the joy drained from Derrick's face and his gaze fixed on the glint of sunlight and steel from an elevated sand ridge 300 yards away. He hoped he was wrong about what he was seeing, or maybe his eyes were playing tricks on him. He hoped he hadn't really seen anything at all out there, but he was a well-trained assistant gunner and he knew how to spot the glass of a sniper's scope. He swallowed hard and clenched his fists.

"Goddamn it," Derrick said.

"Goddamn it who?"

Kevin didn't hear the cracking of the shot, but he saw the glittering red mist blooming from Derrick's left temple and the subsequent explosion that tore through his right ear and jaw, showering Kevin's face with vital fluids and tiny shards of bone. Derrick spun on his heels and fell with full force into Kevin, knocking them both to the ground behind the cover of the semi's front tire. Moments later, the mighty roar of exploding 50 caliber rounds ripped through the heavy desert air and thousands of 5.56mm shells tinkled and clattered down the sides of the gun trucks like a deadly rain, flooding the ground. Rocket propelled grenades detonated over the convoy, forming a mass of black clouds that dumped shards of searing metal and, for a moment, blocked out the punishing Afghanistan sun. Kevin stayed prone behind the cover of the armored vehicle and stared with wide, unblinking eyes at the crimson halo that formed around the face of a man with whom he had shared most of his life. Derrick's brow furrowed hard and then slowly relaxed until a final rasped breath escaped his throat.

Kevin finally blinked. The long stretches of blowing sand and military vehicles that surrounded him blurred and gave way to the greenery of a hillside cemetery. The members of his platoon, all gritted teeth and blazing rifles, were replaced by silent headstones, and the howling scream of incoming artillery shells drowned under the late summer chorus of birdsong. Kevin adjusted the bill of his ragged ball cap, cleared his throat, and patted a cold slab of granite, etched with a simple cross that marked the grave in front of him. Below the cross, several lines of text offered a remembrance:

DERRICK M. WALTON
SGT US ARMY
K.I.A. AFGHANISTAN
SEPTEMBER 10, 1981 – OCTOBER 31, 2008
BRONZE STAR
PURPLE HEART
FOREVER HONORED
LOVED BY ALL

"Hey, man. I've been home a couple months now. Sorry I ain't come out to see you sooner, but I'm all fucked up about this whole thing," Kevin said. "I guess I still ain't forgave you for going out on me like that."

Kevin sat down in the grass and leaned back against the rough side of the monument, pulling his hat down over his eyes. He crossed one ankle over the other and exhaled heavily.

"Hope you don't mind I lean on you a little while. I don't figure you would. It's about time you was more solid than me."

He undid a couple of the pearl snaps on the front of his denim shirt and opened it to fan himself, revealing the sweaty white tank top underneath. It was new and clean, which Kevin hated. He figured if a man's clothes stayed bright white, it was a sign he didn't work nearly hard enough.

"I swear to God, it seemed like our guys littered that ridge for hours." Kevin made his thumb and forefinger into the shape of a pistol and popped off a few mock rounds into the air. "I didn't think they'd ever stop. When they finally did, nobody returned fire. Got 'em, I guess. Or maybe they squirted, but I hate to think the motherfuckers who took you away are still out there. Sgt. Keene had to kick the dog shit out of me so I'd snap out of whatever kind of trance I was in. He got me over to my wrecker and I watched in my side view mirror while they loaded you up in the back of your truck. Everyone on the net was screaming your name, man. They was yelling *K.I.A.! K.I.A.! They fucking got Walton!* Sarge finally convinced them to shut up long enough for one of 'em to call medevac."

Kevin scratched his neck and used the back of his hand to wipe at a single tear that was beginning to form in the corner of his eye. He cleared his throat a few times and sniffed.

"The blackhawks finally found us. Four fucking hours later. I guess somebody called in an air strike, too, but we never saw any. I just heard them cussing about it while we waited. Anyway, the corpsmen laid you on the ground and prayed over you for a little bit while we all paid our last respects. Once nobody had nothing else left to say, they covered up your face with your ACU jacket and hauled you out of there. Keene let me keep your dog tags, which was good of him, and I appreciated it, but we had to finish the rest of the mission with your blood and brains and shit sloshing around in the back floorboard of Bravo 16. I don't know how long it took to finally reach Kushamond, but it was late. Pretty near pitch black. Everybody was doing their best to act normal. Brave, you know? We all crammed into the chow hall and scarfed down BBQ chicken and Afghani cola. I don't know why that particular detail stuck in my head. I remember the dumbest shit."

Kevin laughed.

"That one old medic was bitching about having your blood all over his uniform so I knocked his dinner tray out of his hand and clobbered him. Laid him out cold on the floor for a while. He never talked to me much after that. Probably best he didn't. I was pretty miserable for the rest of the time I was over there. Seven whole months without you. Goddamn."

He pulled the sleeve of his shirt away from his wrist watch and checked the time. Ten 'til two. He pushed the brim of his hat back so it sat high on his forehead, stood to his feet and dusted off his jeans.

"Ahh, shit. I gotta go, man. I hate to up and leave on you, but I'm scheduled for an appointment. They got me seeing a doctor down to the VA hospital every few weeks. Poking and prodding and asking me all kinds of questions a man hopes nobody would ever ask him. Keeping me doped up and all, trying to put me back together, I guess. I got a pill to help me sleep, one to perk me up, one to calm my nerves, and one to make sure I don't just fly plumb off the handle. Well, anyway, good talking..."

Kevin tucked his shirt into the waist of his jeans and headed for the footpath that led down the hill to where he had parked his truck—a 1971 Chevrolet 1500. He swung the door open on its groaning hinges, climbed inside the hotbox of a cabin and turned the key in the ignition. The old pickup cranked a few times before coming alive. Kevin stepped on the gas pedal and the V8 engine's low rumbling swelled to a growl. He rolled down the window, pulled the column shifter into reverse and backed out onto the gravel road. Before he put the truck in drive, he reached for the volume knob on his stereo and cranked it. Jerry Reed was picking his guitar and singing a tune about his adventures trucking illegal booze across state lines. Kevin hummed along as he drove over the hill that led into town.

II

SWIMMING WITH SHARKS

The town of Ash Hill, Kentucky has one main road cutting straight through the middle of it. Deviate from that road too much and it's likely you're trespassing on private property, an offense punishable by a stern crossways look from the owner. Unless they were expecting company. Then they might ask you to come on up to the porch and sit a spell. Ash Hill hardly knew a stranger.

The cemetery was situated just outside of town to the south, and the veterans affairs office sat next to the barber shop, clear up north. Kevin's faded blue and white Chevy kept to the 25 mile per hour speed limit as it rolled along, grumbling and belching gray plumes of exhaust. Business owners who were outside their shops, sweeping the sidewalks or drinking coffee and shooting the breeze, would throw up a hand and offer a friendly wave as Kevin passed. By the time he parked his truck and cut the engine outside the two-story brick VA building, he figured he had been greeted by pretty near a third of the town's population.

Kevin took off his ball cap and laid it on the cracked and faded naugahyde seat next to him. His short-cropped hair was full and dark. His eyes were deep set, but shone a pale blue-green. His face was tan and smooth and clean-shaven, though the shadow of his beard was always visible, no matter how close the cut. He checked his reflection in the rear view mirror. He didn't look like he had been crying, which was all that really concerned him. He stepped out of the truck and hooked his carabiner keychain on one of the belt loops of his jeans. The keys swayed from side to side, jingling as he jogged up the rough concrete steps to the big wooden double doors.

"Hey, Kevin." A pretty young blonde called out from behind the receptionist's desk. Her name was Miranda, Kevin had gathered that much from his few prior visits. Based on the picture she kept on her desk and the set of rings she wore on her left hand, she was married to a god-fearing young man and together they had a little boy. "Dr. Rogers is with somebody else right now, but he should be ready for you in a few. You can go ahead and sign in."

"That's fine. It'll give me time to catch up on my reading." Kevin scratched his name, date and the time down on a clipboard then took a seat on one of the hard plastic chairs, next to a table piled with magazines and informational brochures.

"How you been?" Miranda asked.

"Oh, fair to middlin', I guess. Waiting for something

to come through on a place to live and looking forward to getting back to work. You?"

"In a hurry to get back to work already! You're just something else, ain't you? You checked with Stacy Campbell's dad down to the hardware store? I heard he was looking for somebody to help load feed and soil and stuff after his son got married and moved off to Lexington."

"Not yet. I'll stop through there and see him on my way out. I appreciate the tip."

"Yep. Hey, where you been staying at since you got back?"

"Been renting that little cottage out at widow McHenry's bed and breakfast across the river. Temporary. 'Til paperwork clears on my mamaw and papaw's place and I can stay there."

"How is it? She got it fixed up nice?"

"It'll do for the time being. Gives me a place to lay my head at night and keeps the rain off my shoulders. After thirteen months of bedding down in the desert it really don't take a whole heck of a lot to please me."

"No, I reckon it wouldn't."

Kevin rifled through the magazines on the table beside him. Good Housekeeping, Southern Living, 100 Best Crock Pot Recipes, Field and Stream, Highlights. All several years old. None of them particularly interesting.

"How'd Derrick's blood taste?" Miranda asked. Her voice sounded like a low hiss, full of venom and spite. Kevin shifted uneasily in his chair.

"Do what, now?" Kevin asked. He raised an eyebrow and screwed up his face as he sat taller in his chair, trying to peer over the desk.

"Huh?"

"You just say something?"

"I said I reckon it wouldn't. Talking about it not taking much to please you."

"No. After that. What'd you say after that?"

Miranda pursed her lips and looked confused, her eyes darting from side to side. "Not a thing."

"Oh. Sorry. My ears must be playing...tricks..."

Kevin's ears started ringing, low at first, but it grew louder by the second. The ringing turned to a whistle, and the whistle to a scream. *Incoming!* A blast rocked his brain and his eyes snapped shut. *Pitch black. Pitch black. Pretty near pitch black.* His inner vision washed red. Sweat started building in the palms of his trembling hands. *Knock, knock.* His head throbbed and searing pain stabbed his eyes. *Goddamn it. Knock, knock. Knock, KNOCK. KNOCK, KNOCK!* His hands clenched into tight fists. His head filled with the slow-motion whirring sound of helicopter blades slicing through the air. *Dustoff inbound.* Kevin gritted his teeth. They creaked and groaned under the pressure, like an old wooden bridge, ready to collapse. *Anybody home?!*

"Hey, anybody home?" A short, thick man with a bald head and gray goatee stood over Kevin, snapping his fingers. "Hello!"

Kevin eased open his eyes. The stout man's face was uncomfortably close to his. The warmth and smell of his breath was almost as annoying as his gloved hand lightly slapping Kevin's cheeks.

"Hmm? Yessir, Dr. Rogers, I'm here. Just thinking on something pretty deep."

"Don't think too hard. Doctor's orders," he said. He pulled at the fingers of the latex glove on his left hand. "You can come on back now."

Kevin stood up from his chair, digging his thumb and middle finger into his temples. He squinted hard, blinked a few times, shook his head, and followed the doctor down the hallway toward his office.

"Shut the door behind you and have a seat, if you would. So what's new?" Dr. Rogers took a seat behind his desk and opened a manila file folder. He pulled an ink pen from his shirt pocket and began scribbling at the top of a blank page.

"Same old. Still trying to settle down since I been back. Get used to being a civilian again. Just regular, everyday situations like going to the grocery store can tear up my nerves. I'm always on edge, thinking people are staring at me, waiting for me to do something wrong." Kevin said. He leaned forward in his seat.

"That's all perfectly normal, son. You're used to being suspicious of everyone. You had to be over there. It was a survival instinct. You'll regain your trust." Dr. Rogers smiled and made a few bulleted notes on his paper. "How's your memory?"

"About the same. There's still times when I'll forget whole days. I remember being awake all day, but I couldn't tell you a thing I'd done. And other times when I just don't care much about anything at all. I feel like one of the pills y'all give me is making me lazy. I started calling it my don't-give-a-shit pill."

"Recovery from brain trauma can take time, but most of my patients have regained all functionality in the long run. Don't worry yourself too much, just keep doing your books of puzzles and keep your mind working." More notes. "Now what about your sleep patterns? Have they improved?"

"I, uhhh. Well, I've been sleeping a little bit better, which is good, but I'm starting to take headaches, and they're just awful. I can't hardly function with one." Kevin looked down at the floor and noticed his right foot was tapping on the carpet. He had always been nervous around doctors, whether they were checking his blood pressure or poking him with needles. Something about putting his well-being into the hands of another human being just never seemed right. Humans made mistakes.

"You don't say. About how often are you having them? How long do they last?"

"Started out about twice a week, I guess. Yeah, about twice a week. Now I'm liable to have one every other day or so. There's days where I'll get one of a morning and pack it 'til I go to bed. Other times they'll come on and quit within a minute or two." Kevin looked up at Dr. Rogers and raised his eyebrows. "Tylenol don't do a whole lot for them."

Dr. Rogers scribbled down a few more notes on the paper. He reached for a spiral-bound pad of forms on his desk. Prescription orders. "Well, I can write you a script for migraine medication. Strong pain killer. Just make sure you don't overdo it. No more than one a day."

"Actually, that's something I kindly wanted to talk to you about." Kevin pulled a folded envelope from the back pocket of his jeans. He opened it and removed the paper inside. He slid the paper across the desk toward Dr. Rogers, smoothing out the wrinkles with the palm of his hand. "I went down to the post office yesterday, expecting my disability check. Well, when I opened the envelope, there wasn't no check in there at all. This letter was the only thing."

Dr. Rogers picked up the letter, tilted his head back slightly, and looked down his nose at it. His eyes scanned back and forth across the page and his lips moved slightly, silently mouthing the words as he read.

"What do you make of it?" Kevin asked.

"It's pretty well clear. VA is denying you benefits because they say you're addicted to prescription medication."

"Yeah, that's how I read it, too. But just how in the hell are they going to deny me benefits by claiming I'm addicted to the drugs they put me on in the first place? That don't make a damn lick of sense." Kevin felt a blush come to his face as his cheeks filled with blood and turned warm. A lump grew in his throat. His right foot tapped the carpet harder, the sound of it was audible now. "They was the ones that diagnosed me with PTSD. They was the ones that told me what my symptoms are. They was the ones who pushed the pills on me. Now they're trying to make me out like some piece of shit dope fiend and cut off my pay? Tell me, how can they do that? *How?*"

"The letter says it's a temporary action. If you show signs of improvement and are able to cut back on the medication and still function, they will resume making full payments on your disability claim." Dr. Rogers handed the paper back across the desk. Kevin snatched it out of his hand.

"Isn't that a bunch of bullshit? They put me on the stuff, they got it in my system, and they know I'll be worse off without it now. They set me up to fail! Why didn't you warn me about none of this? I wouldn't have started on it if I'd known this was a possibility. I thought the VA was on my side!"

"We are on your side, son," Dr. Rogers said solemnly.

"We want to see you do well and get back to your old self. This is just standard policy. We see so many people come through who try to abuse the system. It's a safeguard is all. You do what they ask and your checks will return. You haven't been back long, so your bank account should still be doing just fine."

"That ain't even the goddamn point I'm trying to make. Fuck the checks! The point I'm trying to make is I ain't never done drugs in my damn life. Not a one. I took that medication because they told me to, and now they're treating me like I'm a low-life moocher. No. Hell no." Kevin slammed his fist on the desk. Dr. Rogers jumped, then settled back into his chair. "Messing with a man's finances is one thing, but trying to spoil his character is a whole other kind of meanness. They took all the good parts of me they wanted, my loyalty, my honor, my bravery. They took all that out of me and used it for their own. They took my best friend, they took my humanity, they used me up and they shipped me back here and turned me into some kind of damn zombie."

"If you'll just calm down a minute—"

"No I won't. I won't calm down. Not for you and not for nobody. I'm sick of being told what to do and how to do it. So you listen here, and you listen good. The VA can keep their disability checks. And they can keep their damn pills. And they can keep their diagnosis, and their nosey-ass questions, and their puppet strings. They can take all them things and cram them right straight up their ass." Kevin jammed his fist into the air, illustrating his point and painting a vivid picture for the doctor. "I ain't afraid to work for a living, and that's what I intend to do." Kevin stood to his feet. The veins in his neck were thick and bulging.

"I—" Dr. Rogers started to speak.

"If you say another damn word, I swear to God above I'll jerk a knot in your ass faster than you can blink. You and me is done. Our business is over." Kevin shoved the letter into the envelope, folded it, and slid it into his back pocket, never taking his eye off Dr. Rogers. "You'd better pray your ass off before you climb in bed tonight. You better pray the Lord finds you some other line of business, cuz the folks you're working for right now is goddamn devils. Swindling, thieving, crooked goddamn devils."

III

THE ROAD HOME

THE CONCEPT OF HOME WAS SOMETHING KEVIN HAD NEVer fully understood for himself, but for which he had always longed. He had seen what might have been home on television programs. A mother, a father, a kid or two, and sometimes a dog. The shows were all different, but the formula was more or less the same across the board. He had a mother, and she had a kid, but the rest of the puzzle was missing. According to the gossiping old birds around town, and with his birth certificate to back it up, he was a bastard. He must have been an immaculate conception, folks liked to joke, just like the baby Jesus. The truth was, Kevin hadn't been a miracle at all, and he certainly wasn't a blessing as far as his mother was concerned. She wasn't entirely sure who his father might have been. She didn't care.

Katrina was her given name, but most folks around town called her Scratch because of her tendency to dig her fingernails into the pus-filled blisters of weeping eczema that covered her arms and neck. She had developed a number of habits in her younger years, none of which carried with them a bright future, and the things she would offer to do for a couple of dollars would make the Devil blush. She never gave much thought to building a home life for her son, and her habit of betraying anyone who let her get close kept them both drifting from one stranger's sofa to the next. She left Kevin with her parents—his Mamaw Gracie and Papaw Floyd—one gray evening in September and slipped away into the night without a word as to when she planned to return. The police found her body in an abandoned house a week later, two counties over, dead as a doornail with a needle in her arm. They might have never found her if a neighborhood dog hadn't dragged one of her scabrous arms into its owner's yard. They followed the trail and found her decomposing body propped up naked in a corner, the floor all around her littered with soot-stained spoons, used condoms, and puddles of stomach bile.

A little over a month after Katrina's death, Kevin sat in Mrs. Boggs's first grade classroom, working through the week's list of spelling words. Leaf, moon, corn, hay, and a couple of real doozies to top them off—October and pumpkin. The other kids in class were talking about the costumes they would be wearing later that night, and what houses they planned to hit up for the best treats. In all of Kevin's six years on earth, he had never been trick-or-treating. Despite that fact, Kevin loved everything about Halloween. He loved spending the night away from his mother and staying up late with Papaw Floyd to watch monster movie marathons. He loved coloring pages of cartoonish witches and jack-o-lanterns at school, and the smell of candied apples, spiced pies, and dying leaves that drifted through town on the gusts of cool autumn breeze. Most of all, he loved the creepy covers on the storybooks that would be featured in the library's holiday window display, and picking a few to check out and take home to read to his dog. It was the happiest time of the year for Kevin, even if he had never been able to dress up and go around town like the other kids.

School let out with the ringing of the bell and Kevin climbed up the dusty steps of the faded yellow bus—number 16—that took him home every day. The kids inside bounced and leaned with the curves as they wound through the hilly countryside. The trees were mostly naked, with just a few brilliant leaves hanging on to the tips of branches, and sunlight broke through the tangles of limbs and warmed Kevin's face as he stared out the window. Derrick Walton sat next to him, reading one of his comic books aloud and acting out the fight scenes. The rickety, gnarled and knotted bones of faded fence posts jutted from the ground on the side of the road, smothered at their bases by thick patches of weeds, and Kevin watched as they whipped past until the bus screeched to a stop at the end of a long gravel driveway. He stood to his feet and tucked his books under his arm. Derrick didn't miss a beat in his dramatic reading as he slid out of the seat, clearing the path to the aisle. Kevin walked to the front of the bus and hopped down the few dusty steps. An old, speckled blue tick hound was sitting by the mailbox, wagging her tail and sweeping the loose gravel back and forth. She had been waiting for him.

"Hey, Sadie-girl!" Kevin called out to the dog. Her

back legs were wound tight as a spring and they launched her immediately into motion. She bounded toward him, her jowls and loose skin rippling and quaking all over her body every time one of her massive paws struck the earth. Her clumsy frame skidded sideways and collided with his legs, knocking him off balance and forcing him to take a few staggering steps backward. "You big idiot!"

Kevin pushed Sadie aside playfully and ran toward the white-washed clapboard farm house. The driveway hooked around a hill with a big red oak tree in the center and doubled back on itself before ending under a covered car port. Kevin cut through the yard and passed under the tree. When he reached the porch, he bolted up the steps two at a time and flung the screen door open, leaping over the threshold and into the house. He expected to hear the familiar sound of a gospel record hissing and popping on the turntable in the parlor, but the air was dead silent. Normally, his mamaw would be standing at the stove in the kitchen, fixing up the evening's supper and filling the house with the warm aroma of fried foods, but she wasn't there either. She wasn't anywhere as far as he could see.

"Mamaw! Papaw! Y'all home?" Kevin set his books on the entry table. He walked through the kitchen and peeked his head around the corner of the doorway that led into the parlor. The high-backed paisley chair where his papaw always sat while he read the paper and listened to his records was empty. Kevin crossed the room to a set of three large floor-to-ceiling windows that looked out over the back of the property. He pulled the sheer curtains aside and cupped his hand over his eyes, peering through the glass. The scarecrow stood alone in the garden, but there was no sign of his mamaw. The wind blew ripples across the surface of the pond and a few turtles sat on a log, basking in the sun, but his papaw wasn't out there fishing. He started to wonder if maybe they had been raptured while he was in school. He always worried the Lord would show up when he wasn't around. Or when he was on the toilet, taking care of a number two.

Kevin let the sheer curtain fall back into place and turned away from the window. The light that filtered through the fabric was faint and wavy, and it fell across the floor and stretched up the wall of the parlor like shadows of the sun. His heart fell into the pit of his stomach when he saw the pair of figures standing shoulder-to-shoulder in the doorway, blocking the only exit from the room. They stood there tall and silent and unmoving. They wore unfamiliar faces, not those of his dear old grandparents, like he might have expected. These faces weren't even human.

The figure on the left was pale, with mottled blue and purple spots of clotted blood that had formed dark pools under its translucent skin. A heavy brow hooded beady eyes that sunk into impossibly dark sockets—black holes with no sign of light or life in them. All across the forehead was a series of metal rivets, set into its deeply wrinkled flesh and caked with dried blood. The other had a sickly green color to its skin—slick and mean and not of this world. The side of its head had a row of long slits cut into it, starting at the neck and extending up to where the ears should have been. Its lips were red and swollen and it looked like something that had crawled from the bottom of a murky pit of dark water, where no sunlight could ever reach.

Kevin shrank back into the curtains, wrapping them around himself. He heard their heavy footsteps on the hardwood floor—they were coming for him. He knew this day would come eventually—he fully expected it—but he never could have guessed it would be Frankenstein's monster and the gill-man from the black lagoon that would join forces to tear the life from his little body. Dracula and the wolf-man, maybe. That seemed like a more plausible duo to him. Either way, he knew he wasn't long for this world now. He started to pray aloud.

"Dear God, please kill the monsters in my sitting room. I guess they probably already tore my mamaw and papaw to pieces, and I ain't never killed nobody in my whole life, so they deserve to go to Hell, and I deserve to go to church this Sunday. I promise I won't skip it. Thank you, Jesus. I love you. Thank you. Amen."

He could see them through the curtains. They stood over him and extended their long, ragged arms in his direction, clutching at the air with their hungry claws. He braced himself, squeezing his eyes shut tight. Their strong fingers sank into the soft flesh of his pudgy belly, rippling and squirming, feeling for a ripe strand of intestines. And to his surprise, he laughed. They were tickling him. They were tickling him good!

"Lay off me!" Kevin squealed. He kicked his feet and gasped for breath between big bursts of laughter.

The monsters relented, stepping away from their thrashing victim and peeling the skin from their faces. Kevin watched as their hideous features gave way to much more pleasant soft lines and wrinkles. Mamaw Gracie and Papaw Floyd smiled down at Kevin, the masks hanging at their sides.

"Y'all got me. I really was scared for a minute!" Kevin crawled out of the tangle of curtains and stood to his feet.

"'Til you got to tickling me, and I could smell your perfume and chewing tobacco. I was pretty sure who you really was then."

"You ought to seen the look on your face when you first laid eyes on us. I wished I had a picture." Papaw Floyd said.

"They're sure scary masks! Where'd you get them?"

"Down to the drug store. They're some of them monsters from the late-night programs."

"Yeah, I recognize 'em now. Hey, how come you ain't fixed supper?" Kevin put his arms around Mamaw Gracie's waist and hugged her tight.

"Well, I figured we'd go on into town for something to eat tonight. A hamburger or something like. How's that sound?" Gracie asked.

"I like hamburgers! After that, will you read me a Halloween book? I got some new from the library."

"Well, if that's what you want. I kindly figured we'd all go out trick-or-treating in our new masks." Gracie shook the latex gill-man in Kevin's face. His eyes grew wide.

"Can we really? I can dress up and we can all go together?"

"That was the plan."

"Oh man, I can't believe it. Wait'll I tell Derrick. I'm gonna get more candy than him!" Kevin started to run into the kitchen. He paused just inside the door frame and turned around. His face looked serious and thoughtful. "Which one of those masks do I get to wear?"

"How about you go on up to your room and get changed out of your school clothes and we'll talk about it after." Papaw Floyd said.

Kevin rushed up the long set of steps, swinging left

around the sturdy wooden post on the landing and opened the door to his bedroom. Laid out neatly on his bed was a pair of ripped up blue jeans with brown fur sewn into the tears, a flannel shirt to match, and a deluxe werewolf mask from Don Post Studios, just like they advertised in the back of his comics! He changed into his costume and felt a wave of excitement wash over him as he stared at his reflection in the full length mirror. Kevin stalked out of his room, fingers curled to resemble claws and his eyes darting from side to side, looking for tender young prey. He hopped down a couple of stairs, dropped his head back slightly and gave his very best howl. His mamaw and papaw stood at the bottom of the steps, looking up at him, clapping and hooting in approval. They were wearing their masks again, but this time, Kevin wasn't afraid when he looked down at them. This time, Kevin thought to himself about the elusive concept of home. He thought about the families he had seen on television and the formula for home they represented. A mother and a father, a kid or two, and sometimes a dog. And he looked at his grandparents with their masks—Frankenstein's monster and the gill-man standing hand-in-hand with their delicate fingers laced together. And he thought of the Munsters.

A single, salty tear broke free and raced down his cheek until it settled on his lips, spreading out across a great, wide smile. He knew the mask wouldn't betray his emotions, so he let a few more tears slip through. And a few more. And a few more, and on and on until all the sorrows and fears he had been storing deep down inside came to the surface and emptied out of him. It was the best night of his life. He was home.

IV

FROM THE
THUNDER AND
THE STORM

Kevin's blue Chevy pulled into the driveway of his grandparents' house and came to a stop by the mailbox. It had holes rusted through the sides and was barely hanging onto its post by a single nail. The mail hadn't come in quite some time. Sadie wasn't sitting there wagging her tail, waiting for him. She had died when he was twelve years old—run down by a speeding '85 Cutlass Supreme while chasing a gray squirrel across the road. The car didn't kill her, though. Papaw Floyd had to put her down with a shot to the head from his .410. He said there was no way she could have made it, even if he had taken her to the vet. Kevin believed him.

The old gravel road was worn down to the dirt in spots and huge bunches of weeds and tall grass sprung up here and there. The red oak in the middle of the hill stood tall and healthy and proud, a stark contrast to the state of the house itself, which was now covered in creeping vines, green algae, and chipped paint. It hurt Kevin to see.

After Papaw Floyd's first heart attack, the doctor had ordered him to take it easy. He didn't. The house and property was a big point of pride for him and he refused to sit by and watch its glory fade. A second heart attack took him one evening in June as he was cutting the grass with his old reel push mower. Mamaw Gracie found him face down by the pond with one of his hands still on the mower's handle. Their fifty-two years together had come to an end, and she never had the chance to say goodbye. She had faded pretty quickly after that. The cancer set into her bones and whittled her down to nothing. The weariness of the world and the weight in her heart laid her to rest in January.

The day Mamaw Gracie went into the hospital, Kevin drove down to Morehead with his best friend, Derrick Walton, to see an Army recruiter. A week after her funeral, both boys were on a bus, headed for basic training. Derrick did his best to keep Kevin's mind from drifting into dark places throughout MOS training and their deployment. He was good at helping Kevin forget. A year and a half later, Kevin was back, standing on the dusty porch with a set of keys in his hand. The paperwork that granted him ownership of the property had cleared probate court days before, but he couldn't bring himself to make the drive out to the farm. He knew the house would be empty, and he dreaded facing all that nothing. No Sadie. No Mamaw Gracie or Papaw Floyd. No Derrick. Home had slipped away from him and was buried deep in the dirt with a mother and a father, a kid, and a dog.

It was early evening and the summer air was warm and wet and thick with the sound of cicadas. Kevin had awoken that morning with a dull ache in his head, and it had grown over lunch time into a searing pain that threatened to split his skull. He hadn't taken any of his medicine in days. In his stubbornness, he assured himself he could beat the pain in the long run. He was sure he just needed to find a place to settle down and occupy his mind. The sweat in Kevin's palms had made the key slick and he fumbled to turn it in the lock. He wiped his hands on his jeans and tried again. The latch finally clicked. Kevin twisted the knob and pushed the door open. The house gulped in a big breath of fresh air like some frantic drowning thing breaking the water's surface and gasping for life. It had sat unopened for so long, suffocating in the silence, its memories blanketed by a thick layer of dust.

Kevin stepped inside and left the door open behind him. The entryway was mostly unchanged. To the left of the door was the tall entry table where he often stacked his school books as a kid. It was now cluttered with unopened hospital bills and notices from the utility companies. A few had blown off onto the floor when the gust of air swept through the house. Straight ahead of him was the long set of steps that led to the three bedrooms and single bathroom upstairs. An open doorway next to the tall table led into the kitchen. Kevin picked up the bills that had fallen and stacked them on top of the others.

The dining table was set for four and when Kevin saw the empty plates and empty chairs, the incredible weight of loneliness fell over him and he began to cry. Mamaw Gracie had always set the table for four. One for Papaw Floyd, one for Kevin, one for herself, and an extra just in case a guest happened to show up around supper time. You didn't leave Mamaw Gracie's house without being fed. The light in the kitchen dimmed and Kevin could see through the window the weather outside was turning. Darkness crept in from the edges of the sky, threatening to overtake the dying gold and crimson rays of sunlight lingering on the horizon. Purple and white flashes rippled through the storm clouds, followed by distant claps of thunder and a low rumbling somewhere over the hills.

The wind picked up and slithered through the trees, their branches shivering and the leaves hissing. The sun was blotted from view now, and the heavens were a dull grey, like a wash of watery ink spilled over the canvas of sky. The curtain of clouds was charged with pulses of radiance and the electric crackling of thunder filled the air. Kevin's heart beat in his chest and in his skull, thumping in his swollen veins. And the leaves hissed their low hiss, the sky crackled with energy, and his heart thumped. Hiss, crackle, thump. Hiss, crackle, thump. Like the sound of a turntable needle that has drifted into the dead wax at the end of a vinyl record. Hiss, crackle, thump. Kevin remembered the sound. Papaw Floyd would sometimes fall asleep in his chair while listening to one of his gospel albums and Kevin would sit and listen to the hypnotic pattern, watching the needle dance on the end of the tone arm, swaying back and forth, up and down.

Kevin stumbled into the parlor. The disharmonious song of dead wax grew louder and the pounding in his skull made him want to vomit. A loud clap of thunder shook the room and hit Kevin in the top of the head like a ten pound hammer, knocking him to his knees. He could make out the form of the paisley chair through the tears in his eyes, and he began to crawl. His vision had become nothing more than a disorienting blur, and if not for the feeling of the bones in his knees and palms striking the hard wooden floor, he wouldn't have been certain he was moving at all. When he finally felt one of the wooden chair legs brush his shoulder, he pulled himself up and sank back into the cushions.

A barrage of ghostly smells rose from their tombs in the chair's fabric and haunted Kevin's senses—the stench of death and a broken heart. Not the putrid reek of decaying flesh or the earthiness of a fresh grave, but the sweet smell of tobacco and the floral notes of Mamaw Gracie's perfume. The admirable musk of Papaw Floyd's sweat and the acidity of old newsprint paper. The familiar smells of all those things Kevin had held dear, but which were no longer there. They were faint. And fading. And Kevin wished he could die with them.

Rain began to fall outside—the tears of angels. It was slow and steady and soft. The pleasant pattering of each drop on the roof and window panes chased away the drumming in Kevin's brain. The pressure on his eyes abated, too, and took some of the pain with it. His vision grew clearer and his nerves began to settle. He took a deep breath and wiped the agony from his eyes. He blinked a few times and the world around him shifted into focus. That's when Kevin realized he was being watched.

The waves of sheer fabric curtains concealed the true form of the thing on the other side of the window, but Kevin could make out a few of its rough features. It had both palms pressed flat against the glass and its fingers were terribly long and slender. Its head was large, too—radically disproportionate to its apparently tiny frame—and nearly perfectly round. Kevin watched as its fingertips slowly massaged the glass, squeaking and groaning, and the fog of its tiny breaths grew and shrank like a beating heart.

Kevin leaned forward in his seat. The thing jerked its palms away from the window. He started to push himself up out of the chair and the silhouette tensed for a moment before it scrambled out of sight. Kevin leaped across the room and threw the curtains aside. The thing's breath and the outline of its fingertips still lingered on the glass but it was nowhere to be seen. Kevin darted through the kitchen and into the entryway, out the door, off the porch, and around the side of the house. He turned the corner just in time to see the pale set of fingers disappearing beneath the weathered wood of the cellar door. He spotted a fist-sized rock jutting out of the bare dirt around the house's foundation, dug it free, and tip-toed toward the set of double doors on their rusted hinges. The cellar wasn't much more than a hundred square foot dirt hole, so he knew the thing—whatever it was—had nowhere to go. The rain began to fall harder.

A scream broke the silence and stunned Kevin as he reached for the handle on the cellar door. The scream was most certainly human, Kevin thought. And female. But it hadn't come from the cellar. It came from the opposite end of the house. Kevin clutched the rock tighter, his heart pounding. He pressed his back against the house and began shuffling sideways, toward the porch. When he reached the corner of the house, he leaned out far enough to allow his left eye to survey the area. He saw the woman running down off the hill at the edge of his property. She was headed for the house. Her hands and the long, white apron she was wearing were stained deep red. Kevin's mouth filled with a memory he had tried desperately to forget. The sight of all that blood made him weak.

The woman hurried up the steps and onto the porch. Kevin watched her, but didn't speak. Her black hair was wet and it stuck to her face. Under her apron she wore a pair of dark blue-jean shorts and a black tank top. She studied the open door on the house then turned and looked at Kevin's truck. She didn't seem to be seriously injured and she was no longer frantic. She had a few long scratches on her forearms, but there was no way they could have bled enough to have her looking the way she did.

"Hello? Is somebody home?" She knocked on the door and poked her head inside. Kevin stepped out of hiding and walked toward the porch.

"Uhh, yeah. Somebody's home. Just ain't nobody in the house." The woman took a few steps back. She looked at Kevin and smiled. He suddenly became aware of the muddy rock, still clenched in his fist and the fact he was soaked to the bone. He imagined how he must look to a stranger. But then, this stranger didn't look any less suspicious.

"Oh, hey! I didn't see you standing there when I come up on the porch. You live here?"

"Yeah. Just got here today."

"Well, I'm sorry to show up unannounced like this. Glad to have a new neighbor, though. I'm Samantha." She held out her right hand in Kevin's direction and he could see the deep red on her hands was stained, not fresh.

"Are you all right?"

"Huh? Oh, my hands? Yeah, it's just blackberry juice. Scratches are from the thorns."

"Well that's a relief. My name's Kevin." Kevin took her hand and shook it. Her grip was firm, but the skin on her hand was soft and warm. "You come screaming off that hill, looking wilder than a buck and I didn't hardly know what to think."

Samantha laughed. She wrapped her other hand around his and pulled him up onto the porch.

"Says the fella standing out in the rain with a big ol' rock. You fixing to go hunting with that thing? You might ought to lay off it until this storm passes."

"Uh huh. Why was you out in all this?" Kevin asked.

She pulled open the pockets on her apron so Kevin could see. She had blackberries in one and red raspberries in the other.

"Good picking on top of that hill, there. I come out here about once a week to get the ripe ones. I thought nobody lived here, so I didn't figure the berries would be missed."

"Well, you was about half right. I don't got no use for the berries. Wouldn't know what to do with them even if I did take a notion to climb that hill. It's either the birds get at 'em or you do."

"I appreciate it. Maybe I'll fix you a cobbler or something. That storm rolled in on me fast and it started raining before I finished picking. I knew this house was just down the hills, so I figured I'd wait out the storm on the porch. Never expected to meet a new neighbor looking like this." She bent forward, dropping her head and shaking the rain out of her hair. She pulled a black elastic band off her wrist and fixed herself a high ponytail.

"How come you walk all the way out here? Ain't no berries around your place?" Kevin tossed the rock off the porch, into the yard.

"It ain't far for me. I just live over the hill. Your property line butts right up against mine." Samantha untied the apron and slipped it off over her head. She folded it so the berries wouldn't spill out of the pockets. Her tank top was cut low and Kevin found himself staring at her chest. The chill of the rain had raised goosebumps on her tan skin.

"How come I never saw you around town or nothing before?" Kevin turned his eyes to the sky. The rain showed no sign of letting up.

"Oh, we ain't been here long. Just moved in about a year ago. Still, I figured we would have seen each other before now."

Kevin cupped his hand and stuck it out from under the porch roof. It filled with rain and he dumped it. "We? You and your old man?"

"Huh uh. Me and my parents. I ain't married yet."

"Ahh. What's your parents do? Had to be a job that brought y'all into town. I can't see anybody moving here just 'cause." He laughed.

"Mommy's a school teacher. Elementary. And Daddy's a preacher at the Freewill Baptist."

"Oh, Lord. A preacher's daughter? You best take off before your daddy comes looking for you. He sees you hanging around some strange feller and he's liable to skin me alive." Kevin put his hands in the air and took a few steps away from Samantha.

"Or he might thank you for giving me shelter." Samantha took a few steps forward, closing the distance between them. "I see you got a truck there. Mind giving me a ride home, or should I walk back over the hill in all this weather and catch my death?"

"I guess I probably can't let you die, can I? He'd sure take offense to that."

"Okay, then!" She slapped him on the arm.

Kevin pulled the door closed, fished the keys out of his pocket and locked the house. He started down the porch steps, pausing on the last, and turned to look up at Samantha. She reminded him of no one, and he admired her for it. She didn't conjure any memories in him or trigger any old emotions. Looking at her and talking to her was a wholly new experience for Kevin, and he found he didn't want it to end so soon.

"Ready to make a run for it?" Kevin stepped out into the rain and walked toward the truck. He went around to the passenger side and opened the door. Samantha was just coming down the steps and once the rain hit her back, she broke into an awkward, high-stepping run. Kevin felt her hand brush the small of his back as she slid past him and climbed up into the truck's cabin. She reached over her shoulder and pulled the seatbelt down across her chest and buckled it. The rolled up apron lay across her lap and she patted it, looking quite content. "You good now? You situated and got all your parts in place?" Samantha smiled and nodded.

A moment later the truck was starting down the gravel hill toward the road. The wiper blades swiped at the fat drops of rain on the windshield and the high-beams of the truck's headlights lit the way ahead. When they reached the end of the driveway, Kevin stopped and looked at Samantha. He propped his forearms on the steering wheel and pointed both thumbs in opposite directions. "Which way to home?"

"Thatta way." She said, pointing right.

Kevin cut the wheel and pulled out onto the slick blacktop road.

"You always this quiet when you meet someone new?" Samantha asked. Kevin hadn't been aware of the silence.

"No, not generally. I apologize. I've had a lot on my mind for the past little bit and I'm just thankful to not be thinking about it for once, to be honest."

"Like what kind of stuff?"

Kevin sighed. "Well..."

"Never mind. That was rude of me. You just said you was glad to not think about it and here I'm asking you to do just that. Let's talk about something else. What's your favorite color?"

"Ehh. Blue, I guess."

"You guess? You don't sound so sure. Okay, I'll ask you an easy one. What's your last name?"

"Brooks."

"Kevin Brooks. That's a good name. Mine's Jennings. Samantha Sue Jennings."

"That fits."

"How do you mean?"

"It's cute. That's all."

"So you're saying I'm cute? Is that it?"

"I guess."

"There you go guessing again. Am I cute or ain't I?"

"You are. Sorry, I'm an idiot."

"You don't seem like an idiot. Just nervous."

"That, too."

"Well don't be. I ain't gonna bite you or nothing. Turn right on that road up there."

"All right." Kevin turned onto the road Samantha had pointed out. It went on straight for about thirty feet and then dipped down over a hill, out of sight.

"We're the only family that lives on this road, so just

keep going 'til you see my house. You're handsome, too, by the way."

"Huh? Oh, uh, thanks." Kevin rubbed the back of his neck and looked uncomfortable. "Do you like living out here so far?"

"Well look at you! Asking questions and everything. This has become a regular old conversation, hasn't it? Yeah, I like living out here. It's peaceful and the people are nice as can be. How about you? You never said what brought you out here."

"I grew up in that house with my mamaw and papaw. They raised me after my mom took off. I used to love the place, but coming back now, it just seems kindly lonely with them passed away."

"Oh, I'm sorry to hear that. How come you ever left?"

"Military. I was over in Afghanistan up 'til recently."

"Well, welcome home." She saluted him.

Kevin spotted a set of yellow porch lights glowing in the distance.

"There it is." Samantha said. She unbuckled her seatbelt.

Kevin switched the truck's headlights over to the low beams as he pulled up close to the house. Two people watched the truck approaching from the porch—a woman in a rocking chair and a man leaning against the railing. The truck came to a stop and Kevin put it in park but did not cut the engine.

"Well, see you around, I gue—. See ya." Kevin said.

"Don't think you're off the hook that easy. Daddy would never let me speak to you again if you showed up and dropped me off without introducing yourself. And I'd maybe like to talk to you again sometime, so come up to the porch for a minute. Just to say hello, then I promise you can go."

If Kevin was being honest, he would have said he was in no hurry to get back to the house anyway. He would have told Samantha that just before she showed up he had been chasing a small, pale *something* around the house, and he was almost afraid to go home and see it again. He would have told her that, despite being nervous, he had enjoyed talking to her. He turned off the truck, killed the head-lights, and adjusted his ball cap. "All right. Just for a minute. On account of being proper."

Samantha hopped out of the truck and ran up to the porch, wrapping her arms around her daddy's neck. He put his arms around her waist and squeezed her. He stood a full foot taller than Samantha, which meant he had a few inches on Kevin, trim most everywhere except a little round belly. He had broad shoulders and wore a polo shirt tucked into a pair of khaki pants. His hair was neat and combed, parted at the side with bangs that swept down onto his forehead and curled around to his temple. It was clear he was a serious man, dressing to impress, even in the comfort of his own home.

"We was worried about you."

"I'm all right. Our new neighbor here didn't let me stand out in the rain. This is Kevin Brooks." Samantha turned and motioned for Kevin to come up on the porch. "Kevin, this is my daddy, Robert, and my mommy, Kelli."

"Howdy." Kelli said, still rocking in her chair. She had a little extra weight on her frame, but she seemed to carry it beautifully. Her hair was pulled up into a messy bun and she was fanning herself with a magazine. Her cropped capris, red and white striped sleeveless top, and flip flops showed she was perhaps a bit less reserved than her husband.

"New neighbor, huh? Where you moving into?" Robert asked.

"Just across the hill there, sir. My property's the next one over from yours."

"That old white house with the growed up yard?"

"Yes, sir."

"Well good. I bet you'll have that place looking right in no time. I'll be glad to see it fixed up. Where you moving here from?"

"I always lived here, sir. I just come home from Afghanistan not too awful long ago."

"Well, son! We sure appreciate you." He reached out and grabbed Kevin's hand. His gave it a few firm shakes. "It's a pleasure to meet you."

"The pleasure's mine, sir." Kevin allowed himself a slight smile.

"Which church do you belong to?" Robert asked.

Kevin felt his cheeks go flush and his smile fade. He hoped it was dark enough that Robert couldn't see his color change. "I ain't been to church since I got back, sir."

"Well, we'd love to see you start. You're more than welcome at the Freewill Baptist any time. Come on down this Sunday and I'll dedicate a sermon to you."

"Yes, sir. I appreciate it." Kevin checked his watch. "I hate to run off, but I got a few things yet to settle at the house before it gets too late. It was real nice meeting y'all."

"All right, then. Hope to see you down to the church house!" Robert waved as Kevin walked toward his truck. "Thanks for looking after Sam."

"I was glad to, sir. Y'all take care."

"Bye! See you soon!" Samantha called out and waved excitedly.

The tail lights on Kevin's truck glowed red and he backed out of the driveway. As he pulled away he gave a few short toots on the horn and then he was gone. The Jennings family stood together on their porch and watched him go. When they could no longer hear the low rumbling of his truck's engine Robert turned to his daughter and smiled.

"He seems like a nice young man. Good, level head on his shoulders."

V

VENUS IN PISCES, MOON IN CANCER

THE SHORT DRIVE HOME SEEMED TO TAKE FOREVER. KEVIN couldn't keep his mind away from how foolish he must have sounded. He thought of Samantha and how she had looked, soaked and stained and disheveled. She was gorgeous just the way she was, but Kevin knew he was in for real trouble if he should ever see her in her Sunday best. She thought he was handsome. He didn't know what to make of that either. He imagined how she would laugh if she found out he had never even kissed a girl. *Yes ma'am, I've killed more than twenty men, but I'm terrified of women.* What a joke, he thought.

The house was hot. Miserable hot. Kevin went upstairs to his old room, which was now nothing more than a twin size bed pushed up against one of the walls. There were no sheets, pillows, or blanket on the bed, but that suited Kevin just fine. He wouldn't need them with the house scorching like it was. He peeled off his wet t-shirt and dropped it on the floor. That didn't bring him enough comfort so he added his jeans to the pile.

He hadn't even bothered to turn the lights on in the house. For one thing, he knew every inch of it like the back of his hand, and the lightning outside was now a pretty constant display of purple pulses—heat lightning—which was rarely ever accompanied by thunder. He fell onto the bed face first and stretched his limbs across the mattress, his hands and feet dangling off the edges. He turned his head to look out the window at the light show in the sky.

Was Samantha getting ready for bed, too? Kevin imagined she was. He imagined she would strip out of her wet clothes, just as he had, and admire the curves of her own body in the mirror. He pictured her wearing a matching black lace bra and panty set. In his mind she unclasped the bra and let it slide down the smooth skin of her arms and fall to the floor. Her hands cupped the undersides of her teardrop breasts, squeezing them gently, fingers pressing into the soft, warm flesh. Her thumb and middle finger tugged at her tender, pink nipples, pinching and teasing them. Kevin imagined they would grow hard, and he realized he had done just that.

She pulled up her vanity bench and set it directly in front of the mirror. The cool fabric of the cushion would feel nice on the warm, firm flesh of her perfectly round ass as she sat down and spread her legs. Her tiny fingertips with their deep red stains would glide up her legs and sink into the warmth between her thighs, pulling her panties to the side. The middle and ring fingers on her right hand slid up inside her body and her left hand massaged her swollen clit. Every delicate fold grew wet and slick and she arched her back, waves of raven hair cascading over her shoulders. She felt a hunger growing within her and she thrust her hips forward, forcing her fingers deeper inside.

Samantha's right hand slipped from between her legs, bringing with it all the fluid of her passion. Silver strands of nectar stretched between her fingers, glistening in the light. She turned her gaze to the goddess reflected in the mirror, staring deep into her own eyes, and took all of the wetness into her mouth. The familiar taste of her sex mixed with the lingering sweetness from the berries on her tongue. She moaned, swallowed, and sent her hand back for more. She curled her fingers inside herself, pressing hard against the wall of spongy flesh just beneath her pubic hair, as if her reflection was pulling her off the bench toward it. She gave in and fell to her knees on the floor, rising and falling, gliding up and down along the full length of her twitching fingers.

Her left hand pressed harder on her clit and made quick little circles all around it. The pressure building inside her had her aching for release. Harder and faster she fucked herself. Harder and faster she massaged her eager clit. Harder and faster until she felt the levee inside her break and release the gushing flood. Quickly, her fingers slid out of her, followed by a torrent of clear liquid, running down her legs. Her body shuddered and she fell back. Her frantic breathing was the only sound she heard, gasping in perfect rhythm with the throbbing between her legs.

It might go something like that, Kevin thought. It might go nothing like that. It didn't really matter to him. It was his fantasy and he was in love with it.

Across the hill, Samantha was thinking of him, too. She remembered the sadness in his eyes and how nervous he had been. She fantasized about running her fingers through his hair and she imagined a look of absolute calm and peace came over his face. She might kiss his forehead gently, and he might sigh and melt into her caring arms.

Together they drifted off, each tucked in with their own fantasies of the other. Kevin couldn't believe what he was feeling in those few moments before sleep took him. The swiftness of his beating heart, the tickle of energy flowing through his extremities, the mounting urge to laugh at nothing in particular. He was excited. He was happy.

It was watching. It saw everything, and it hated him.

VI

AS ROMANS

"The good Lord moved in me this weekend, brothers and sisters. He surely did. He spoke to me and inspired me and I knew I had to share this story with y'all." Robert looked out over his congregation from the pulpit. His Bible lay open before him, turned to the book of Romans. A simple wooden crucifix was mounted high on the wall above a baptism pool. His eyes scanned the faces in the crowd as he preached, but he lingered when he saw Kevin and Samantha, seated next to one another.

"Samantha was out and got caught in the thunderstorm that passed through that evening. A young man brought her in out of the rain and he gave her a ride home. Now, when I saw that truck pull into my driveway and I watched my only daughter step out of that thing with a good looking young stranger..." An uneasy smile spread across his face and he laughed. "Well, folks, I don't believe I got to tell you just how I felt."

Kevin felt Samantha's hand brush his leg. She picked a piece of lint from his pants and smiled.

"Well, after I got to talking to this young man, I come to learn he was a soldier, just home from Afghanistan. It's no exaggeration, brothers and sisters, when I tell you all those feelings of apprehension and fear just went right out of me. The Lord had let me know Samantha was in good hands. His hands. This young man knew how to fight. He knew how to win wars." Robert slipped on his reading glasses and searched with his finger across the open pages of the Bible. "And you might all be saying to yourselves *Pastor Robert, that's all fine and well, but he's back home now and there ain't no more war to fight.* And to that I would reply with Romans chapter 7, verses 22 and 23." He read aloud. "For in my inner being I delight in God's law; but I see another law at work in me, waging war against the law of my mind and making me a prisoner of the law of sin at work within me."

Kevin leaned forward in the pew, his full attention directed at what was coming next.

"We're all fighting a war, you see. Every day of our lives, we're locked in that deadly battle with sin. Material desires. Temptations of the flesh. It don't ever quit. No matter how we try, we've all got some kind of war going on inside us." He flipped to a new section in the bible. "James chapter 4, verse 1 asks us: What causes fights and quarrels among you? Don't they come from your desires that battle within you?" Robert took off his glasses and laid them on his bible. He stepped out from behind the pulpit and began to pace.

The question made Kevin's bones ache. The fear set into his muscles and his entire body was tense. War was never-ending. There was no escaping it. Derrick's lifeless face flashed in his mind. Sweat broke on his brow and he felt the urge to run. Run from that place and run from Robert's truth. When he thought he'd had enough and he should stand up from the pew and excuse himself he saw it. He could see its features clearly now. Pale, damp skin hanging loose over a pitiful skeleton. Deep black holes for eyes, two rough slits for nostrils, pencil thin lips that stretched across most of the width of its bulbous head. It wore no expression as it peered at Kevin from the baptism pool. He looked at the people around him and everyone's attention seemed to be focused on Robert, all nodding heads and praying hands and amen. They were entranced.

"How will you fight the war inside you?" Robert continued to probe. "A soldier knows sacrifice. He has faced hardships and trials, but he remains dedicated to the fight, and he always finds a way to overcome. To complete his mission and defeat the enemy. But he doesn't do it alone, folks. Soldiers work as a team. They give each other strength! Second Timothy chapter 2, verse 3: Join with me in suffering, like a good soldier of Christ Jesus. Ephesians 6:11: Put on the full armor of God, so that you can take your stand against the devil's schemes! Praise the Lord! I'd ask you to join me today, brothers and sisters. Join me in the army of righteousness and holiness so that together we might win that war against sin. Let us all hold hands and pray." Robert closed his eyes and bowed his head.

Samantha grabbed Kevin's hand as she bowed her

head. The feel of her touch calmed him, waves of tranquility washing over his rattled nerves. As he bowed his head he looked toward the baptism pool and saw the thing sinking out of view. He closed his eyes and he prayed for the first time since he was a little boy.

"Lord, we thank you for this beautiful day. For bringing us all together here and allowing us to share in your love and your grace and in your word. Lord, we would ask that you move in any heart here today that has not come unto you and asked to be saved. Help them and guide them and give them the strength to be a soldier for the kingdom of Heaven. It is in your holy name that we ask these things, Jesus. Amen."

The crowd echoed the amen, raised their heads, and began to chat amongst themselves. Most of them moved toward the back of the church toward the double doors, but a few stood and talked with their neighbors. Samantha let go of Kevin's hand and he felt his heart sink.

"So, what did you think? Not as bad as you expected?" Samantha asked.

"It was good. Lot of truth in what he was saying." Kevin smiled at her. He was right about seeing Samantha in her Sunday best. She wore a bright green sundress with a white cardigan and a necklace strung with different sized and colored beads. If she'd worn shoes into the church she had kicked them off in a corner somewhere because she was barefoot now. Once a few people had cleared out of their row, she crossed her legs under herself and leaned toward Kevin, propped up by her left arm across the back of the pew. Her hair hung in loose curls, framing her gentle face. If she was wearing any makeup, it was minimal. Her skin looked smooth and fresh and she had an overall glow about her that made Kevin feel lighter than air.

"You look real nice in your uniform." Samantha ran her index finger along Kevin's collar. His formal Army Service Uniform was the only thing he had even remotely resembling dress clothes, so it seemed his only option. "You always wear it when you gotta dress up?"

"Not if I can help it. It was either this or blue jeans and a work shirt. I'll go into town later and get a couple nice pairs of britches and a shirt or two." Kevin said.

"Hmmm. Suit yourself. I like it." She touched the tip of Kevin's nose with her finger and he went cross-eyed to play along. They both laughed.

"You care to walk with me a minute? I figured on having your daddy give me the grand tour." Kevin nodded toward Robert who was standing in front of the pulpit, shaking hands and chatting with the people as they passed.

"Good idea. I think he'd like that!" Samantha seemed excited. Her facial expression shifted into a cartoonish look of scrutiny. "You just trying to score points with the preacher man?"

Kevin scoffed playfully "What on earth kinda fella you take me for?" He winked at her and started toward the pulpit.

"There he is! Glad to see you could make it, son!" Robert met Kevin with a friendly handshake.

"Yessir, I wouldn't miss it. You delivered a powerful message."

"Thanks to you! You were a real great inspiration."

"It's a real nice church you got. Mind if I poke around and get an eyeful?"

"Not one bit! Everybody's pretty much cleared out. You make yourself at home and I'll run back to the office and finish up the paperwork and booking and all."

Kevin walked around to the side of the stage and ascended the few steps. Samantha sat on one of the first row pews and looked up at him.

"Look at you up there. You look like you belong."

"Reckon?" Kevin asked.

"Come from a whole line of preachers, I figure I ought to be good at spotting one by now."

Kevin pretended to take interest in the finer details of the pulpit's scrollwork, but he kept the baptism pool in his peripheral vision. He turned to face it and his heart jumped up into his throat. It pounded in his head. Every step he took toward the water seemed to take an eternity, and his feet felt impossibly heavy.

"You been baptized?" Samantha asked from the pew.

"Yeah..." Kevin was close enough now that he could see the ripples on the water's surface. "When I was...nine." Kevin looked into the pool and saw the pale, round head with its black, cavernous eyes looking up at him from the bottom. He jumped back and let out a choked yelp. He took a few slow steps away from the water, his eyes locked on, waiting to see the hideous thing break the water's surface and come for him. Before he realized what was happening, Samantha was moving past him.

"Don't!" He barked. It was too late, she had already leaned over the edge of the pool.

"What is that?!" Samantha screamed. He watched in horror as she sank further into the pit, her hands thrashing in the water. A moment later she jerked her body upright and staggered back on her heels. When she turned to face him, he could see her hands were wrapped around the frail, white thing. Its wrinkled skin dripped and the bulbous head lolled from side to side.

"Baby doll!" Samantha exclaimed. "Somebody drowned the poor thing trying to baptize it!" She laughed and laid the child's toy on the pulpit. She shook the water from her forearms and sniffed. "Probably one of the Wednesday night youth group kids pretending to be a preacher and playing baptism. They're cute like that."

Kevin's heart was racing and he felt embarrassed and relieved all at once. He looked at the naked baby doll and gave a nervous laugh. "I can't believe I jumped and hollered at that. I feel like a heel."

"Nah. It just surprised you is all. The water played tricks and made it look a whole sight bigger than it is. I would have hollered, too." Samantha said. "That'll be a fun story to tell later."

"You wouldn't." Kevin said, trying to look menacing.

"I would. I will. Daddy will get a kick out of it."

"That's all right, I didn't need my dignity anyhow. Not as long as I got you around to whip all my monsters for me."

Samantha put up her dukes and bounced up and down like a boxer from the thirties. "Let me at 'em! Let me at 'em!"

Robert emerged from the back room with his Bible and study book under his arm. "What are y'all cutting a shine over out here?"

Kevin started to fess up, but Samantha cut him off. "I saw that old baby doll at the bottom of the baptism pool and it like to scared me to death." She gave Kevin a sideways glance. He didn't think it was possible for her to get any cuter than she already was, but smug looked good on her.

"Huh. Some little kid is probably missing that thing

right about now." Robert said. "Hey, Kevin, you got plans for later on this evening?"

"None to speak of. I gotta run into town and pick up a few things, but I'm free other than that."

"Good, good. Me and Kelli would like to have you out for supper, if that suits you."

Samantha looked at her dad and smiled. "Somebody's got a crush!"

"You hush!" Robert looked embarrassed. "It's good for me to have another feller around to talk to once in a while. Between you and your mommy you've plumb wore me out on baking and crocheting and such."

Samantha squinted and stuck out her tongue.

"So what do you think, Kev? Can we set out a plate for you?"

"Yeah, I might could eat a bite or two. I appreciate the offer. You need me to pick up anything from town?"

"Yeah, could you run down to the gettin' place and pick up a new attitude for my daughter? I think she's wore hers out."

"I'll see what I can do." Kevin grinned at Samantha.

"Supper ought to be ready around six or so. You can head on out whenever you take a notion, though."

"Yes, sir. I'll see y'all then."

VII

BREAKING BREAD

IT WAS HALF PAST FIVE IN THE EVENING WHEN KEVIN'S OLD blue Chevy pulled up outside the Jennings' home. He no longer wore his formal suit. While he was in town he had stopped by the department store and picked out two pairs of slacks—one black and one khaki—and one of each color polo shirt. Tonight he wore all black. Samantha had heard him pull up and she ran to the door to greet him.

"Well, I didn't know Johnny Cash was coming to dinner!" She looked him up and down.

"Yeah, well, I ain't too sure about which colors looks good together, so I played it safe."

"You're cute. Get on in here." She still wore her church clothes, minus the cardigan. Her shoulders were pink and dotted with freckles. Kevin considered saying something about being jealous of the sun because it had clearly kissed her shoulders, but he thought better of it and decided to keep it to himself. Save that one for the second date, he thought.

Kevin looked around the living room. "Y'all got something against vampires?" He asked.

"How do you figure?"

"Crosses." Every wall was decorated with at least three crucifixes. In a few places there were clustered arrangements of 5 or 6 in different sizes. "Vampires can't stand 'em."

"Oh. Ha-ha. Dad's a preacher, remember?"

"Oh, that's right." His voice was thick with sarcasm. He snapped his fingers. "That explains it."

Kevin noticed a couple of fishing poles and a sizable tackle box tucked into a corner near one of the cross-clusters. He pointed. "Your daddy like to fish, too? Can I be that lucky?"

"Those are mine, thank you very much." She started toward the kitchen.

"Hold on. Wait. Stop right there."

"What is it?" She looked over her shoulder.

"I gotta tell you something. It's pretty important."

"Okay. Go on." She was intrigued.

"These two old dry pieces of fish meet on top of a mountain. One looks at the other and says 'long time no sea.'" His expression was dead serious.

She turned her head to face the kitchen again, but she didn't move. She stood in place, silent. And then she doubled over, arms crossing over her stomach, and she howled with laughter.

"Yep. Keeper." He patted her on the back as he walked by.

In the kitchen, Kelli was transferring a fried green tomato from a hot pan to a cooling rack. The smell of home cooking filled the air and Kevin felt a hard lump forming in his throat as his mind flooded with memories. He swallowed hard and pushed past the thoughts.

"Smells delicious," he said.

"Why thank you! Supper will be ready directly. Bob is on the back porch, if you want to go on out there and say hello." She pointed toward the door with her spatula.

Kevin looked out the back door and saw the preacher reclining in a chair with his feet propped up on the railing and an acoustic guitar on his lap. He was strumming it lightly and humming to himself. Kevin stepped out onto the porch.

"Evening, sir."

"Sure is! You don't gotta call me sir, though. Bob will do."

"Bob it is."

"You pick?" Bob took his feet down off the railing and turned to face Kevin.

"Some. Me and my papaw used to pick along with his gospel records." Kevin pulled up a seat.

"Suits me. Get that old Martin over yonder."

Kevin picked up the guitar and strummed it. He plucked each string, and adjusted the machine heads when one sounded like it needed tuned. When he'd finished tuning the high E he strummed it again and nodded in approval. "What's an easy one to start?"

"Now hold on, son. Don't get ahead of yourself. You gotta warm up first." Bob reached under his chair and fished out a mason jar half full of a clear liquid. He took a sip and offered it to Kevin. "This ought to do it."

Kevin looked confused.

"What? 'Cause I'm a preacher I can't take a drink of the evenings?"

"I was kindly thinking something like that. Not that I'm judging, I just ain't never seen such a thing." Kevin reached out and took the jar.

"Behold the rain which descends from heaven upon our vineyards. There it enters the roots of the vines, to be changed into wine. A constant proof that God loves us, and loves to see us happy."

"Paul write that?"

"Huh uh. Ben Franklin. But that don't mean they's any less truth in it."

Kevin took a drink from the jar. It burned his lips and his stomach and everything in between. He grimaced and handed the stuff back. "I don't believe that's wine in the jar, Bob."

"Po-tayter, po-tahter." He took another sip. "Let's hit a lick on something slow to start. Little Cabin on the Hill suit you?"

"That's a good one. You start and I'll come in."

Samantha watched from the kitchen. Bob set the tempo and called out the chord changes. Kevin followed along and tried to solo when it came around to him. They both took turns singing verses and they'd belt out the chorus together. Kevin's voice was better than Bob's, but Samantha would never tell her father so. It warmed her heart to see the two of them getting on like they were. It warmed her heart to see Kevin wear a genuine smile.

They shared another drink and started in on the next

song. When that one was finished they whet their whistles and played something a little faster.

Kevin began hitting sour notes. And his tempo seemed to drag in spots and rush on others. Samantha watched as the smile fell from his face and his expression turned grave. He kept staring at something just off to his left. Samantha looked out across the yard but she saw nothing. She figured the moonshine and Kevin's nervousness was getting the best of him, so she stepped out to relieve him.

"All right, Flatt and Scruggs. Supper is about done. Y'all get in here and wash up."

Kevin set the guitar in the spot where he had found it and stood to his feet. He walked toward Samantha, looking back over his shoulder once and then squeezing past her into the house in a hurry. Bob took it slow, whistling as he went. His face was bright red and sweat gathered on his face and chest.

"You okay, Kev?"

"Yeah. Just hungry is all. I ain't eat all day and I took a dizzy spell out there." Kevin rubbed his stomach. When Bob had moved past him, he shut the door and looked out over the yard again. Samantha took him by the arm. He turned to see her smiling sweetly up at him and he finally felt the pleasant tingle of the moonshine set in.

He went over to the kitchen sink and washed his hands before sitting down at the dinner table.

"This seat okay?" Kevin asked.

"It don't matter. I'm sitting next to you, whichever one you pick." Samantha said.

Samantha helped her mom set the table and Bob took the seat directly across from Kevin. They half smiled at one another.

"Buzzed?" Bob asked.

"Pretty well." Kevin admitted.

"Good. Lead the blessing for us, would you?"

Everyone bowed their heads but Kevin. He looked at the three of them with their eyes closed and decided it wouldn't be worth protesting, so he started to pray over the food. "We thank you, Lord, for the blessings of the day and the food on this table. Thank you for the kindness of strangers and them not being strangers no more. For watching over us and keeping us from harm, Lord. We thank you for family and togetherness. And for those without no family, let them find home wherever they break bread. In Jesus name we pray, Amen."

"Amen, son!" Bob's eyes lit up. "I don't know about y'all, but I feel blessed!"

Dinner was everything Kevin had hoped it would be. Soup beans with chunks of thick-cut bacon, fried potatoes, cornbread, and green tomatoes. Bob served up more than a few helpings of embarrassing and adorable stories about Samantha on the side.

"I think that's about enough story time for one evening," Samantha said. "If y'all would excuse me for a minute." She stood up from the table and disappeared around the corner into the kitchen. She returned a few moments later carrying a baking dish. She set it on the table and Kevin could see it was blackberry cobbler.

"Dessert this evening comes courtesy of Mr. Kevin's berries." Samantha cut a square from one of the corners and served it to Kevin. He took a bite and chewed thoughtfully.

"Well, if I had knowed this is what could come of them berries, I'd have been getting them myself a long time ago. I'll have to get the recipe off you."

✎ "Or... I'll keep that to myself and just give you a reason to keep coming around," Samantha scowled. "Now hurry and finish up. We got to walk it off."

When Kevin had cleaned his plate, Samantha pulled him up out of his chair.

"Shouldn't we help clean up first?" Kevin asked.

"Oh, no, y'all go on ahead. I'll take care of this," Kelli insisted.

"Where you goin' with my boy?" Bob finished the last bite of his cobbler.

"Figured I'd take him back on the property and show him my path over the hill." Samantha pulled at Kevin, dragging him toward the back door.

"Y'all be safe. And behave." Bob raised an eyebrow at them and laughed.

The sun hung low in the western sky, glowing a deep orange, and turned the forest around them into a mono-chromatic landscape. As soon as they were beyond the view of the house, Samantha took Kevin's hand and dug her heels into the ground, stopping abruptly, and spinning him around to face her. She kissed him. Her eyes were closed, but his were wide open. He had hoped they would share a kiss someday. He had daydreamed about it. But he hadn't expected it then. There. A million thoughts raced through his mind, and he panicked. He had practiced kissing on his arm in the privacy of his bedroom many times, but it hadn't prepared him for this. This was softer. Sweeter. It meant something.

"Is everything ok?" she asked, looking at him with concern.

"Yeah. I'm just..."

"Nervous?"

"When am I not?" Kevin shrugged.

"I've been waiting to do that all day, you know. Since I saw you in church this morning."

"I've been waiting to do that my whole life."

Samantha's eyes grew wide and a playful smile spread across her lips. "You mean... No..."

"Yeah, I ain't never kissed a girl. So what? Big deal." He pouted, kicking at the dirt.

"You are something special, Kevin Brooks. Here." She took his hand and led him over to a sycamore tree. She leaned against it, pulling him close. He was hesitant.

"You're about the sweetest thing there ever was, but you keep me so gaddang tore up all the time, and I can't figure out what's up and what's down. I don't want you to think–"

Samantha moved her hands up to his shoulders and pulled him closer. She placed his hands on her waist and he felt helpless to object any further. Her fingers slid up the back of his neck and gently tilted his head to the side. She brought her face closer to his and whispered. "Shhh. Pay attention."

He could feel Samantha's breath on his lips. She moved slowly and deliberately, allowing him time to absorb the lesson. Kevin closed his eyes when he felt her lips press against his. He was ready this time. He marveled at the duality playing out between them. Samantha's lips were soft, but they kissed him firmly. Her intentions pure and innocent, but fueled somewhere underneath by a hunger for flesh and the pleasures it could provide. Kevin's mind drifted back to the morning's sermon about the battles we fight within ourselves. He thought of all those people who were faltering, laying down their arms and letting the struggle consume them. And he found himself in the middle of a brand new war. He had become possessed by Samantha's very being.

Her milky skin smelled like honey and vanilla, and her lips were sweet and red—the cherry on top. She ran her tongue lightly across his bottom lip and moaned. He thought of how she had looked in his fantasies. He thought of the things she had done. How could anyone hope to fight a war against something they wanted so badly to win? Her hand slid up his leg and grazed the tight spot in his pants. He was flying the white flag of absolute surrender. She moaned louder when she felt he was hard and she grabbed him.

Kevin's eyes startled open. He saw it. It had been lurking there the whole time—he could feel its watchful gaze on them. Any time he had seen the thing before, its face was expressionless, but now it was angry. He pulled Samantha away from the tree, put one hand on her shoulder and the other on the small of her back, and rushed her back down the trail toward her house.

"Kevin! What on earth are you doing? Stop!"

"I want to keep going with you, I really do, but not like this. Not here. I don't want anyone to see us." He had told half the truth. He didn't think she would believe the other half.

"I'm sorry. I hope I wasn't being too forward. I just—" She sounded sad.

"No. *God no!*" He assured her. "I wanted it. Every bit of it. I want it now, but I can't. *We* can't."

"I just got caught up..."

"I know. Me, too, trust me. I just don't want to disrespect your daddy's place. If you don't plumb hate me after this and we ever get there again, I want it to be in the right place, at the right time. I'm afraid if I let myself stay out here with you and we keep on like we was, I won't be able to stop myself."

"I couldn't hate you, Kevin. You're respectful to a fault, and I'm an absolute mess over here, but I understand where you're coming from. And I appreciate you feel that way."

They broke through the edge of the woods and stepped onto her lawn. Kevin glanced back at the trail behind them, but the thing wasn't there. He slowed his pace.

Inside the kitchen, Bob and Kelli were finishing up the last of the dishes.

"I like him." Bob said.

"I know you do."

"Don't you?"

"I do. And so does Samantha."

"Is it bad if that don't bother me in the least?"

"I don't think so. You've always been a pretty good judge of character."

"She deserves to be happy. I've seen the way she lights up when he's around. It's like—"

"Like she used to look at you when she was a little girl?" Kelli gave him a knowing glance.

"Yeah. Like that."

"Speak of the devil. Here they come." They watched as Kevin and Samantha walked through the yard and up onto the porch.

"Do you gotta go already?" Samantha whined as they came through the door.

"Probably I do," Kevin said. "I've got to get an early start on my house tomorrow. Pretty well sick of it looking like they ain't nobody living there. Neighbors will start calling me lazy." Kevin gave Bob a wink.

"I put together some of the leftovers for you to take home." Kelli said, handing him a plastic grocery bag stuffed with food saver containers.

"And I put you something a little extra in there." Bob smiled. "Careful with it. Don't hurt yourself."

When Kevin got home and unpacked the bag he found the half-empty jar of moonshine with a note that read *Thanks for the inspiration.*

VIII

HEAD GAMES

SAMANTHA SHOWED UP A LITTLE AFTER MIDNIGHT, JUST LIKE she had promised. Kevin heard her soft footsteps moving through the ankle-high grass as she approached, but he pretended to be scared when she grabbed him from behind and shouted in his ear. He had been standing at the edge of where the garden used to be, looking down the hill at the pond. The dark water limned a mirror image of the brilliance in the night sky. She wrapped her arms around him and began kissing his neck and shoulders.

"Sorry about earlier this evening." He turned to face her. She was dressed for bed, with blue and white flannel pajamas and her hair pulled back into a ponytail. Her top was only half buttoned, exposing the tops of her breasts.

"Make it up to me?" Her voice was low and soft and sweet. "You remember what I taught you?"

"I can't see myself ever forgetting that. It's all that's been on my mind."

"Show me."

Kevin took her face in his hands. He tried to control his trembling, but the way she looked at him sent tremors through his entire body. He closed his eyes and moved in to kiss her. His lips brushed hers and she gasped, drawing out his breath. Kevin felt proud at how well he could recall the motions. He was a quick study.

"Very good," Samantha said. She took a step back and looked up at him, biting her lip. "Now let's change it up a little bit."

"Okay." He swallowed hard.

Samantha laid down on the grass and slipped her fingers into the elastic band of her pajama bottoms. Kevin watched her slide the flannel down her legs. He froze in place, staring at her naked flesh, pale as the moonlight. She placed a finger on her clit and tapped it a few times.

"Here. Kiss me here." Samantha reached up and took Kevin by the hand, pulling him to his knees. She wrapped her legs around his waist and worked them up his back. Kevin felt himself falling forward until his face pressed into her stomach. She put her hands on the top of his head and pushed him down. He lingered for a moment, pushing all doubt from his mind. Then he began.

Kevin showed no signs of apprehension now. He explored every inch of her inner thighs, eager to learn which areas made her react. He listened to her body and followed every unspoken direction. What Kevin lacked in experience, he made up for with intuition and intense passion. He was surprised at how quickly she came. Her legs tightened around his head, holding him in place, focusing his attention in just the right spot. She moaned and they writhed together. Kevin's excitement grew and his attention became more firm. She came again. Her moans swelled to a scream.

Kevin felt the heels of Samantha's feet digging into his back as her jerking became more frantic. She screamed louder and began kicking. He felt the pain in his ribs from the barrage, but his mind was elsewhere. He never wanted to stop. Samantha's howls fell to a groan and all the tension left her body. Kevin felt her legs slide off his back and fall to the grass at his sides. He never expected that he could give her such pleasure. Her pussy was slick and swollen and he gave it one final, soft kiss.

"Was that okay?" Kevin asked. His eyes drifted up the length of her body and saw the thing. It stood above her head and licked at a trickle of blood running down its pallid forearm. Where its skin had once hung loose on its frame, it was now taught. What Kevin would have described as a pitiful creature when he first laid eyes on it was now lithe and mean. The soft flesh beneath Samantha's chin lay wide open, trails of crimson running down the sides of her neck and pooling in the center of her chest. Kevin tried to find his voice to scream, but he was choked by the frozen lump of fear growing in his throat.

The thing lunged at him. Kevin lowered his head to dodge the attack and his face buried in the warmth between Samantha's legs. It landed on his back and spun. The creature sank its long fingers into the back of Kevin's head, forcing his face deeper into Samantha and cutting off his breath. It tore into the skin at the base of Kevin's skull, clawing and digging to find his spine. He reached back and grabbed at its raking hands. He felt the warmth of his own blood running down his temples and into his ears.

The thing struggled to break free of Kevin's grasp, but he held strong. It screeched and sank its teeth into Kevin's neck where it had been digging. Kevin released its hands and began scratching at the soft flesh on its bald head. He felt his fingernails dig in and tear away at its clammy skin. His ferocity grew and he tore at the thing harder, trying to take it apart.

Kevin became aware of the searing pain in the back of his head. Every chunk of skin he tore out of the thing caused him agony and he realized his own fingers were pressing into his wounds. He thrashed and shook his whole body wildly. He felt the weight of the thing lift from his shoulders and he pushed himself up into a sitting position. He rolled over onto his hands and knees and raised his head, ready to lunge into action and finish his assault. The thing was gone. Kevin stared at a mattress, soaked through with blood. He blinked hard and looked around at the bare, gray walls of his bedroom.

"Goddamn you!" Kevin pounded his fists against his knees and screamed. He stood to his feet and walked across the room to the window. He looked out at the garden and the pond, but there was nothing there. No dead Samantha. No creature. "What the fuck do you want from me?!"

A wide column of moonlight pushed its way through the room and illuminated Kevin's naked body. He stepped away from the window, breathing heavy and looking at his hands. They were smeared with thick, sticky blood. He touched the back of his head and found a ragged, gaping hole. He clenched his fists and felt the blood squish between his fingers. From somewhere inside the room, he heard it laughing.

IX

PIECE OF MIND

MONDAY

So I reckon it can touch me after all. I was starting to think it wasn't even real. I thought maybe laying off them drugs had me all turned sideways. Up 'til now it just watched me but never got close. It caught me when my guard was down. When I was sleeping. I spent the rest of Sunday night and on into this morning sitting on my bed and waiting for the sun to come up. I could hear it somewhere off in the room licking itself. Cleaning up my blood, more than likely. When the sun finally showed and lit up the room, it was gone. At least I couldn't see it. I get the feeling it can see me, though. I hope Samantha and her family is okay.

TUESDAY

I'm doing my best to get rid of every place it could possibly hide. I cleared all the vines off the outside of the house. I cut the grass real low, too, and I boarded up the cellar tight. Nailed a bunch of old planks across the door to where nothing can get in or out. I keep candles lit in every corner of whatever room I'm sitting in. I can't stop picking at the back of my head. It hurts real bad and stinks to high heaven, but the pain is doing a good job of keeping me from falling asleep. Every time I feel myself nodding off, I pull a little piece out of the hole and jab it with my finger a while.

WEDNESDAY

I'm dizzy. I listened to a couple of papaw's records today. Late last night I felt myself trying to drift off so I started painting the house. The moon was bright enough I could pretty well see what I was doing. It didn't really matter, I just needed to keep moving. I smell Samantha. I think it's her perfume on my clothes. Sad. I just fu...

It's in here.

THURSDAY

My ears won't stop ringing. I think I fell asleep. I hit my head on the table. Blood. More blood. Did it touch me again? I made up my mind to tell Samantha about it today. I was scared, but I knew she would help me. She would believe me. I think. I couldn't go because it was standing at the door. It don't want me to leave. I think

FRI

Oh. I see.

S

Got you. No more.

X

HOLLY SUE NATION

SAMANTHA HADN'T HEARD FROM KEVIN ALL WEEK. SHE AS-
sumed he must have been busy with the house and didn't
want to bother him. Every time she drove by, she noticed
that it looked a little better, but she never saw him out
working on it during the day. She figured he must have
been working at night, when the sun was down and it was
cooler. She wished she would catch him out just so she
could stop and tell him how good the place was looking.
To spend a few minutes with him. It didn't happen. She
reassured herself that Sunday was coming, and she would
see him in church.

Sunday came and Kevin didn't show. Samantha's head
filled with nightmare scenarios that involved Kevin getting

hurt or accidentally killing himself in various unlikely ways. She told herself if she had just stopped by and knocked on his door, maybe she could have saved him. She didn't hear a word of Bob's sermon that morning. Her heart was beating too loud.

"Y'all mind dropping me off at Kevin's house on the way home from church?" Samantha asked. "I ain't heard from him all week and I just want to make sure he's okay. I know he's been working on his house, but a man needs a break. And something to eat."

"You're a sweetheart, sissy. Good woman." Bob hugged her.

They picked up lunch from the market in town. It was wrapped up in a brown paper bag and Samantha had written Kevin's name on it with a red permanent marker. A heart dotted the i. She clenched it in her fist as she walked up Kevin's driveway.

She took the steps two at a time and knocked on the door. No answer. She knocked twice more. No answer. She walked around to the back of the house and looked out at the pond, but Kevin wasn't anywhere to be found. His truck was there, but everything inside the house was silent and dark.

Samantha started up the hill toward the berry bushes, figuring she'd take the shortcut home. She turned to look back at the house and spotted Kevin sitting on the edge of the roof.

"Kevin?" She shouted. "What on earth?" She trotted back down the hill a bit and looked up at him. He didn't speak or look her way. "We missed you in church this morning." He was silent. "I figured I'd stop by and see how you were doing." He turned his head slightly and shifted his eyes to look at her. His face was expressionless. "Are you hungry? I got you a couple of sandwiches and a sack of chips from town."

"You best go home," Kevin said, his voice dry and distant.

"What? No! Kevin, why are you treating me like this? What did I do to you?"

"You didn't do nothin'. Just go home. Let me be."

Samantha squinted her eyes to get a better look at him. She could see that his face was covered with dark stubble and his eyes were tired. She was used to seeing sadness there, or nervousness. Now she saw nothing. It scared her.

"You look like you ain't slept in forever. Kevin, are you okay? Please come down here and talk to me."

Kevin shifted uncomfortably when she mentioned sleep. He almost looked afraid for a moment, but then he pushed all hints of emotion from his face. "I told you once, now I'll tell you again. Go. Home." He slid down the roof toward the front of the house. He hung his feet over the edge and lowered himself down until he felt the window sill. He slipped in through the opening and Samantha watched as the window closed and the curtains drew together. She cried the whole way home.

Inside, Kevin sat on the floor in his mamaw and papaw's old room. The wallpaper was patterned with vines of ivy and different flowers. The floor was covered with an ornate Persian rug. In Kevin's eyes everything was alive. The patterns lived and breathed and moved. The lines and colors bled off their respective surfaces and into one another. He could see things hiding in the vines, watching him. He could hear the walls breathing and the thing skittering somewhere behind them.

He hadn't slept more than a few minutes at a time since the night of the attack. He shunned food and water. He knew he would die soon. And he knew that his own death also meant the death of the thing. He had figured out the link between them sometime between Thursday night and Friday morning. He thought back on all the times he had seen it. It watched him cry over the dining table setting and the smells in the chair the first time. It appeared next in the church when he felt scared at the thought of never-ending war. It had watched him smile on the back porch with Bob and squirm with anxiety in the woods. And it touched him when he was feeling so many things in his dreams. It was feeding on his emotions. Growing stronger.

Kevin was stricken with absolute terror when he considered that it might go after Samantha. He had seen the anger and hatred on its face when she kissed him. He couldn't take the chance of letting it hurt her. It had to be weakened, and if it was feeding on his emotions and gaining strength through him, Kevin would starve it. He emptied himself of all feeling. He was a husk. It hadn't shown itself in days and Kevin was beginning to scrub the image of its face from his memory. And then Samantha came by. Kevin had watched from the roof as she walked up the gravel driveway, happy and nervous. It was back. It was watching her. When the tears began welling up in her eyes and the sadness set in, Kevin saw the thing smile. He'd be damned if he would let it hurt her.

Kevin knew he would sleep tonight, and every night hereafter.

The barbiturates had done a great job in helping Kevin sleep when he was still taking them. The VA doctor loaded him up with a two month supply to start, and Kevin was now glad that he did, seeing those mountains of addiction and death poured onto his plate at the dining table. He was in a trance, crushing each pill, one by one with a spoon, chopping it finely with his driver's license, and pouring the powder into the half jar of moonshine. When he had finished with the last pill, he screwed the lid onto the mason jar and shook it. The cloudy liquid swirled inside. He picked up the note Bob had written him and flipped it over. He scrawled something quickly on the blank side and shoved it into his pocket.

Kevin stepped out onto the porch. The sun had gone down a little more than two hours ago, but the night air was still hot and damp. He walked down the driveway and when he got to the road, he turned right and followed it around the hill toward Samantha's house. He walked slowly and deliberately, his face locked in a blank stare. When he saw the porch lights lit up on the front of the Jennings' home, he felt the urge to turn around and walk back home without following through with his plan. He stopped and studied the house for a few minutes. The windows were all dark. He walked up on the porch and slipped the note under the door, then he started back toward home. He hesitated a few times, stopping on the side of the road, and considered going back and snatching up the note. It took him three hours to finally make it to his driveway. Once he saw the house, he knew there was no going back.

Upstairs in Samantha's room, her bed was empty and cold.

XI

BY BLOOD AND

FIRELIGHT

WHEN KEVIN STEPPED ONTO HIS OWN PORCH HE SAW CANDLE-light flickering in the kitchen. Tremors tore through his limbs and it took all his concentration to stop his hands shaking enough to turn the doorknob. He smelled vanilla and honey as he stepped through the door.

Samantha sat at the kitchen table. The jar of moon-shine was open in front of her, and a little more than half of the liquid was gone. Tears streamed down her face when she looked up and saw Kevin walk into the room.

"Hey. Hope you don't mind." She motioned toward the jar. Kevin stared with wide, unblinking eyes. His heart pounded. "I got here a couple of hours ago. You weren't home, so I came on in and figured I'd wait for you. Helped myself."

Something inside Kevin broke and he began to cry. He walked over to the table and picked up the moonshine. He took a drink.

"Well, I guess there ain't really nothing I can do about it now. Just let me have the rest, will you?" He coughed and sniffed as he pulled out a chair and took a seat at the table.

"Drink up, I don't care. Just talk to me." She reached over and brushed the tears from Kevin's cheek. "I've missed you, and I'm so scared..." she paused to take a deep breath. "...so scared that you're trying to put me out of your life." Her eyelids sagged.

Kevin heard it breathing from a shadowed corner in the parlor. Samantha was going. Her breathing was slow and labored, but she was still conscious and talking. He hoped he had enough time to say what needed to be said.

"I love you, Samantha. If I've known you for a week, I've known you all my life." He took another drink and smiled as it burned his throat.

"Love ain't disappearing and shutting me out. That is *not* how you love somebody, Kevin." She pushed back from the table and stood to her feet. She was visibly weak. She walked into the parlor and Kevin followed, picking up one of the candles.

"I know. Not normally. But I had to push you away for your safety and mine."

"That's bullshit! That's the same old kind of line I've heard time and again. I'm sick of being lied to like that! Tell me the truth, Kevin. If you really love me, tell me the goddamn truth!"

Kevin saw it take a step out of the shadows. It wanted him to see.

"I don't guess the truth will hurt anything now." He

looked back to Samantha who had moved across the room and was now slumped in the paisley chair. Her breathing was barely perceptible. Kevin walked over and sat on the floor. He laid his head in her lap. "There's something in this room with us right now. It's watching us from that corner over yonder and it's waiting for what's coming. It wants me keep right on loving you."

Samantha ran her fingers through his hair, just as she had done in her fantasy. Kevin opened his heart and let himself feel everything.

"Love..." she whispered. Her movements were weak.

"Yeah, baby. Love. And sadness, he wants me to feel that, too. And I am sad. I'm sad that I could never love you like I wanted to. Like you deserve. I'm angry because I dragged you into all this, and I should have told you about the thing that's been haunting me. I'm angry because you're dying right now and it's all my damn fault."

Samantha wheezed.

The thing stepped fully into the moonlight and Kevin saw it. Its skin was pink now and it looked almost alive. Its eyes burned with hatred and love and fear and hunger for more.

"And I'm afraid, Samantha. I'm afraid because I love you and because I'm angry with you and because I know that nobody will understand a damn thing when they find out what I done. They'll all say I was crazy and that I murdered you and they'll say I deserve to burn in Hell. I'm afraid because that thing right yonder has got a hold on me that I can't break. And I'm afraid that when we're gone it'll go on and get ahold of somebody else."

The thing kneeled behind Kevin. It licked and sucked at the hole in the back of his head. Kevin put his hand on Samantha's chest. She wasn't breathing anymore. He picked up the candle and held it near her face. She looked peaceful and beautiful and the last hint of a smile remained on her lips. Kevin tilted the flame of the candle toward her and it leapt from the wick and into her hair. He watched as the fire grew and spread to the paisley chair. He dropped the candle on the floor and lay back down in Samantha's lap. The thing still licked him and so did the flames. He wrapped his arms around Samantha's waist and hugged her tight.

"I love you so much."

XII

TO ONE FAR AWAY

Bob Jennings shuffled through his living room with a cup of coffee in his hand, heading for the rocking chair on the front porch. He yawned and opened the door. A small slip of paper drifted across his foot and settled on the floor. He leaned down and picked it up. *Thanks for the inspiration* was written on the front, in what he recognized as his own handwriting.

"Hmm," He said. He flipped the paper over and saw a message scrawled across the back.

PLEASE FORGIVE ME

ABOUT THE AUTHOR

Rachel Autumn Deering is an Eisner and Harvey Award-nominated writer, editor, and book designer from Columbus, OH. She has written for DC/Vertigo Comics, Blizzard Entertainment, Dark Horse Comics, IDW, and more. Her most notable works are *IN THE DARK, CREEPY, VERTIGO QUARTERLY,* and *ANATHEMA.* Deering lives with her wife, two dogs, and a collection of monster masks.

Visit her online at www.rachelautumndeering.com.

Made in the USA
Columbia, SC
25 July 2020